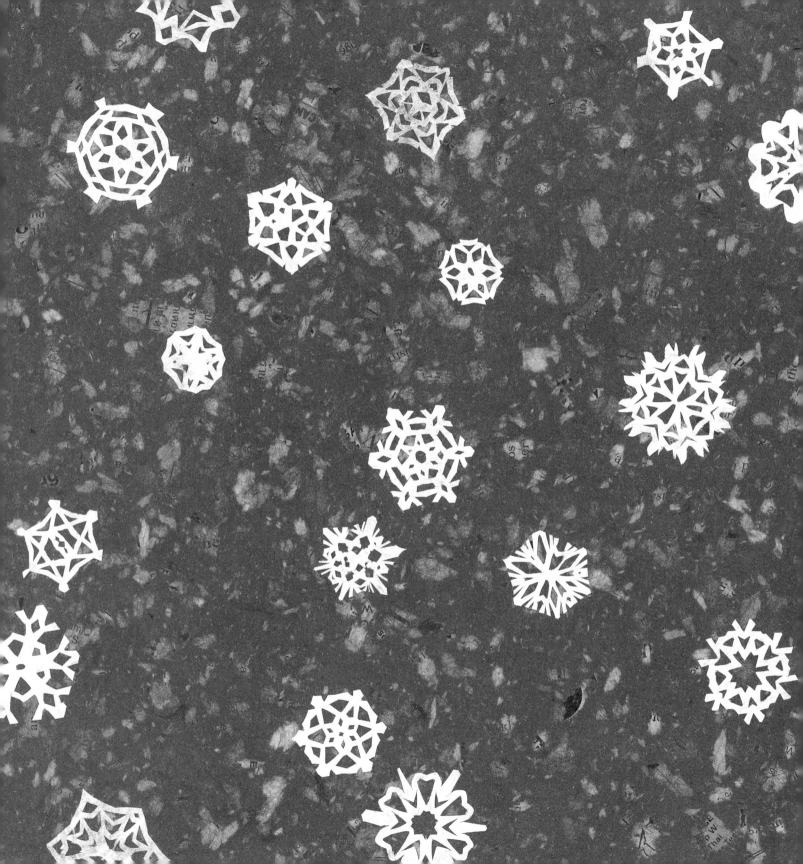

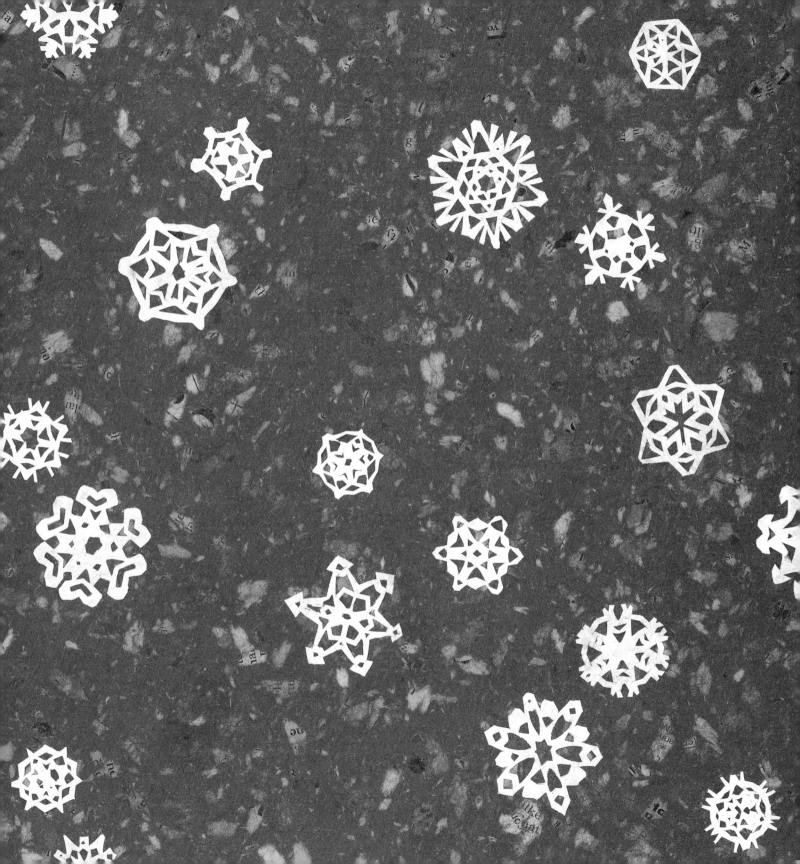

To my son, Ryan, the best gift I ever received,
and in memory of his Nana, my mother—
who always made the days leading up to Christmas
the very best times of the year — T. S.

SQUARE
FISH
An Imprint of Macmillan

SNOWBEAR'S CHRISTMAS COUNTDOWN. Copyright © 2004 by Theresa Smythe.
All rights reserved. Printed in August 2009 in China by South China
Printing Co. Ltd., Dongguan City, Guangdong Province.
For information, address Square Fish, 175 Fifth Avenue, New York, NY 10010.

Square Fish and the Square Fish logo are trademarks of Macmillan and
are used by Henry Holt and Company under license from Macmillan.

Library of Congress Cataloging-in-Publication Data
Smythe, Theresa.
Snowbear's Christmas countdown / Theresa Smythe.
Summary: During each day of the month of December, Snowbear prepares for and celebrates the Christmas season.
[1. Christmas—Fiction. 2. December—Fiction. 3. Bears—Fiction. 4. Counting—Fiction.] 1. Title.
PZ7.S66493Sn 2004   [E]—dc22   2003023527

ISBN: 978-0-312-58141-1
Originally published in the United States by Henry Holt and Company
Square Fish logo designed by Filomena Tuosto
First Square Fish Edition: 2009
Designed by Amy Manzo Toth
1 3 5 7 9 10 8 6 4 2
www.squarefishbooks.com
The artist used cut-paper collage to create the illustrations for this book.

Theresa Smythe

SNOWBEAR'S
CHRISTMAS COUNTDOWN

SQUARE
FISH

Henry Holt and Company
New York

It was the month of December
and time for Snowbear to get
ready for Christmas.

On the **1**st day he wrote a list of all the presents he wanted Santa to bring him.

Snowbear
computer
thanks
skis
paints
telescope
bee hive
snowshoes
ice cream maker
pretty good.
because I've been
Here's my list
Dear Santa,

Santa Claus
101 candy cane
North Pole

Gran

On the **2ⁿᵈ** day he took his favorite wool hat and scarf out of the storage closet and checked them for moth holes.

On the **3**rd day he strung a cord of brightly colored lights along the roof.

On the **4**th day he arranged his collection of snow globes on the mantel.

On the **5**th day he wrote and mailed all of his Christmas cards.

On the **6**th day he shoveled a path from his house because it had snowed the night before.

On the **7**th day he made a snowman.

On the **8**th day he made ornaments
out of paper, glitter, and glue.

On the **9**th day he picked out a Christmas tree and brought it home to decorate.

On the **10**th day he set up his toy trains.

On the **11**th day he went Christmas shopping.

On the **12**th day he wrapped all his presents for his family and friends.

On the **13**th day he went sledding down the giant hill near his house.

On the **14**th day he caught a cold and had to stay in bed.

On the **15**th day he watched his favorite holiday movies and snuggled under the blankets.

On the **16**th day he cracked nuts
with his new nutcracker.

On the **17**th day he hung
a wreath on his door.

On the **18**th day he bought a poinsettia plant to brighten up the kitchen.

On the **19**th day he had Charlie over for lunch.

On the **20**th day he ate too many candy canes and got a bellyache.

On the **21**st day he went caroling with his friends.

On the **22**nd day he went ice-skating
and counted the stars.

On the **23**rd day he hung up his stocking and read a book by the fire.

On the **24**th day it was Christmas Eve, so he made a plate of cookies for Santa and his reindeer.

And on the **25**th day, with the help
of all his friends, he had himself a
very **Merry Christmas!**

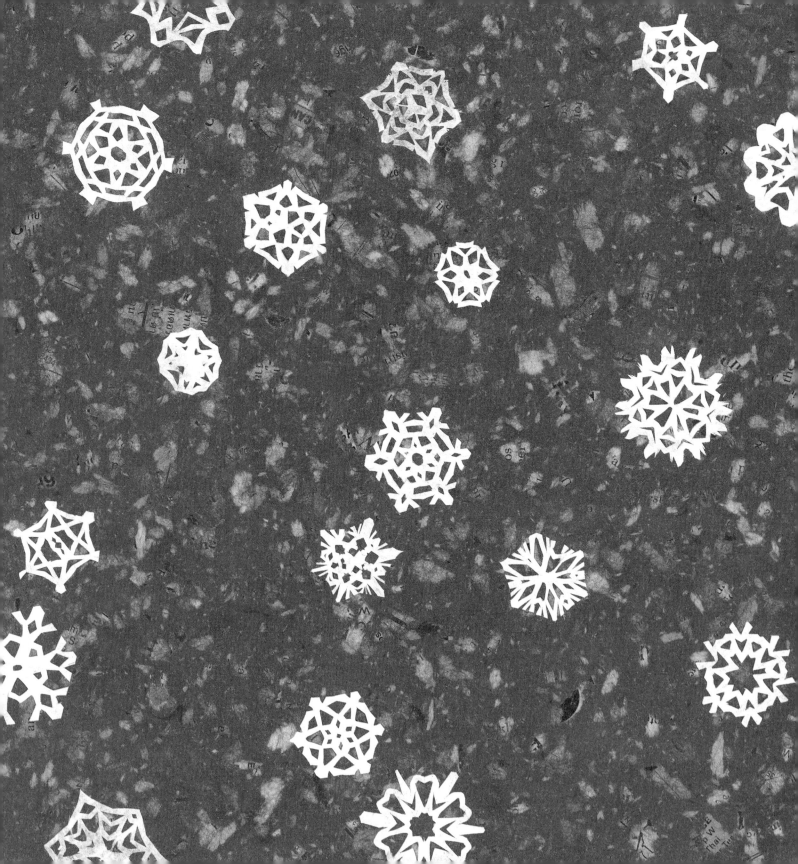

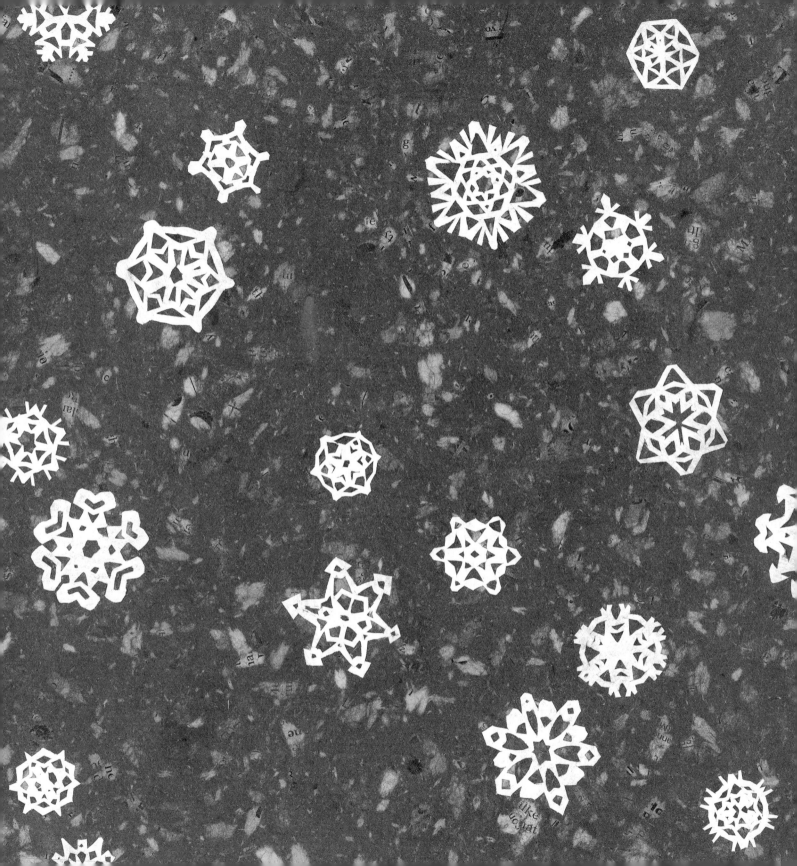